C000046033

ROGER AWAY!

HarperCollins*Publishers*

HarperCollins*Publishers*
77–85 Fulham Palace Road,
Hammersmith, London W6 8JB
www.harpercollins.co.uk

Published by HarperCollins*Publishers* 2008
1

www.rogertheweb.com

The Authors assert the moral right to
be identified as the authors of this work

A catalogue record for this book
is available from the British Library

ISBN 978 0 00 723256 7

Printed and bound in Great Britain by
Clays Ltd, St Ives plc

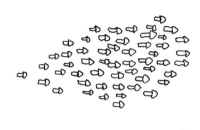

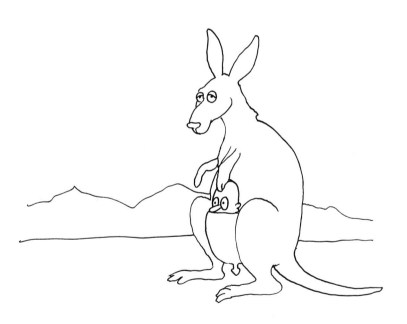

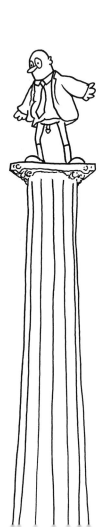

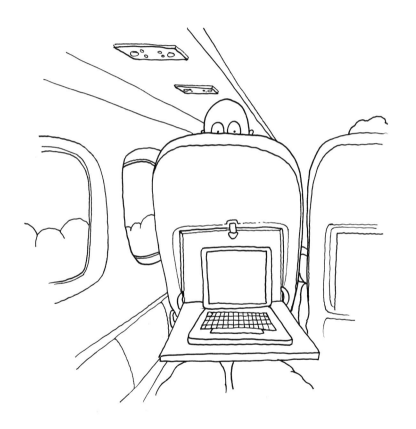

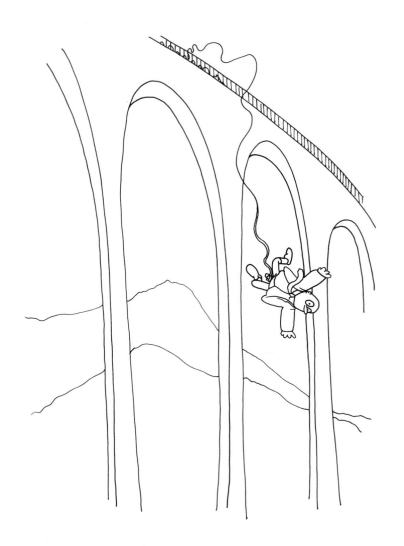